Read Grandpa Spanielson's
first Chicken Pox Story:
The Octopus

A Snout for Chocolate

by Denys Cazet

Grandpa Spanielson's
CHICKEN POX STORIES
story #2

📖 HarperCollins*Publishers*

Grandpa Spanielson's Chicken Pox Stories: Story #2: A Snout for Chocolate Copyright © 2006 by Denys Cazet All rights reserved. No part of this book may be used or reproduced in any manner whatsoever without written permission except in the case of brief quotations embodied in critical articles and reviews. Printed in the United States of America. For information address HarperCollins Children's Books, a division of HarperCollins Publishers, 1350 Avenue of the Americas, New York, NY 10019. www.harperchildrens.com

Library of Congress Cataloging-in-Publication Data

Cazet, Denys.

A snout for chocolate / by Denys Cazet.— 1st ed.

p.   cm.— (An I can read book) (Grandpa Spanielson's chicken pox stories ; story #2)

Summary: When Barney gets chicken pox, Grandpa tells him a funny story to keep his mind off his itching.

ISBN-10: 0-06-051093-5 — ISBN-10: 0-06-051094-3 (lib. bdg.)

ISBN-13: 978-0-06-051093-0 — ISBN-13: 978-0-06-051094-7 (lib. bdg.)

[1. Storytelling—Fiction. 2. Grandparents—Fiction. 3. Dogs—Fiction.] I. Title. II. Series.

PZ7.C2985Snu 2006

[E]—dc22

2004030197

CIP

AC

1 2 3 4 5 6 7 8 9 10 ❖ First Edition

Janey,

Nellie,

Toby, and

Mr. Biggles

Grandma closed

Barney's bedroom door softly.

Grandpa poured himself

another cup of coffee.

"How's my favorite grandpup doing?"

he asked.

"Better," said Grandma.

"Doctor Storkmeyer says

he needs plenty of rest."

"What he needs," said Grandpa,

"is another one of my famous

anti-itch chicken pox stories!"

8

Grandma held up a bucket.

"Windows," she said.

"Windows?" said Grandpa.

"Windows," said Grandma.

"You said you'd wash them today!"

9

"That was before Barney

got the chicken pox," said Grandpa.

"He's resting," said Grandma.

"You can't do two things at once.

You're not as young

as you used to be!"

"Nobody is as young

as they used to be," said Grandpa.

Grandma raised her right eyebrow.

"Windows," she said.

She handed Grandpa the bucket

and pointed at the door.

"Windows first, story second."

Grandpa sighed.

Grandpa carried the bucket

out to the garage

and filled it with soapy water.

He looked at the ladder.

He looked at the bucket

of soapy water.

He looked up at Barney's window.

Grandpa smiled.

"HA!" he said. "Who says I can't do

two things at the same time!"

Grandpa carried the ladder

back to the house.

Grandpa climbed up
and opened Barney's window.

"Grandpa!" said Barney.

"What are you doing?"

"Shhhh," said Grandpa.

"I'm washing windows."

Grandpa washed the window.

"Done!" he said.

"How are you feeling?"

"Itchy," said Barney.

"Time for one of my famous
anti-itch stories!" said Grandpa.

"Be careful, Grandpa," said Barney.

"Ladders can be dangerous."

"Not for a fireman," said Grandpa.

"Did I ever tell you about the time

I saved Mrs. Piggerman's life?"

"You mean the Mrs. Piggerman

who lives next door?" Barney asked.

"Yep," said Grandpa.

"We got the call at lunch time."

A Snout for
Chocolate

nce upon a time,

in the olden days,

when Grandma washed

her own windows,

I was the fire chief.

We were sitting around

the firehouse when the phone rang.

19

A voice said, "'Elp me! 'Elp me!"

"Who is this?" I asked.

"Msss 'Iggy-man," said the voice.

"Icky man?" I said.

"You're an icky man?"

"NOOO!" shouted the voice.

Doc Storkmeyer listened.

"Who is this?" he asked.

"Msss 'Iggy-man! I 'uk!"

"Piggerman!" said Doc.

"It's Mrs. Piggerman and she's uk!"

"'Urry!" cried Mrs. Piggerman.

WOOOOOO

I sounded the alarm.

Sirens wailed.

Red lights blinked.

Two fire engines

and an ambulance roared

to the Piggermans' place.

Strangely, when we got there,

we didn't see any smoke.

I sent the boys around back

to check out the house.

Doc and I went up to the front door.

It was open.

We went in.

Stay here!

?

Check the back!

There was a pile of candy wrappers
on a little table.

"Lunch?" I said.

"Shhh," said Doc. "Listen!"

Someone was calling softly.

It sounded like "'Elp me, 'elp me."

It was coming from the kitchen.

Uh-oh! Someone
is off her diet.

We looked.

Mrs. Piggerman

was in the refrigerator.

At least part of her

was in the refrigerator.

The front half

was in the refrigerator.

The big half

was still in the kitchen. **WHOA!**

Mrs. Piggerman's head

was in the freezer.

Her snout was stuck

to a frozen box of chocolates.

Doc looked at me.

I looked at Doc.

"She's stuck!" I said.

"How are we going to get her out?"

"Hammer?" said Doc.

"'ELP!" said Mrs. Piggerman.

"Blowtorch?" I said.

"'ELP! 'ELP!" said Mrs. Piggerman.

Doc found a hair dryer.

I blew hot air across

Mrs. Piggerman's nose.

The ice started to melt.

"Get ready!" I yelled.

"She's coming loose!"

"'Oo hot on me 'ose!"

Mrs. Piggerman shouted.

"Froze?" I said.

I turned up the heat.

"'ELP! 'ELP!"

cried Mrs. Piggerman.

"Timberrrrrrrrrr!"

Hold on!

someone yelled.

"Move her out!"

Doc shouted.

It would have been easier

to move the refrigerator.

It took all of us to get her

out of the house and down the steps.

After a few minutes in the sun,

the box of chocolates slid off her nose.

I passed the chocolate around.

Mrs. Piggerman jumped up
and snatched the box away.
"MINE!" she yelled.
She stomped into the house
and slammed the door.

"Wow!" said Barney.

"I don't know why she was so mad," said Grandpa.

"Doc Storkmeyer ate all the creams. All I got were those chewy things that stick to your teeth!"

"You'd think she'd be more grateful," said Barney.

"You'd think so," said Grandpa. "How are the itches?"

"Getting better," said Barney.

"It's my anti-itch stories,"

said Grandpa.

"Did I ever I tell you about the time

Doc Storkmeyer and I

got lost in the jungle?"

"No!" said Barney.

"Yep!" said Grandpa.

"Doc Storkmeyer

got his head shrunk by cannibals."

"Shrunk?" asked Barney.

"Shrunk!" said Grandpa.

44

"Shrunk to the size of a cranberry!"

"Wow!" said Barney. "Tell me!"

"Well . . . once upon a time—"

Suddenly the door opened.

Grandpa ducked down.

Barney grabbed a comic book.

Grandma came in

and sat by the window.

"I made some cocoa," she said.

"This will make you feel better."

"Thank you," said Barney.

Grandma smiled.

"I made myself one too," she said.

Barney looked at the tray.

There was a third cup on it.

"Who's that one for?" he asked.

Grandma picked up the cup

and held it out the window.

"Guess who?" she said.